Timmy's
SCHOOL
SURVIVAL
Handbook

by Sarah Willson

SCHOLASTIC INC.

New York   Toronto   London   Auckland   Sydney
Mexico City   New Delhi   Hong Kong   Buenos Aires

Based on the TV series *The Fairly OddParents*® created by
Butch Hartman as seen on Nickelodeon®.

ISBN 0-439-66667-8

12 11 10 9 8 7 6 5 4 3 2 1   4 5 6 7 8 9/0

Printed in the U.S.A.   40

First Scholastic printing, September 2004

And these are my fairy godparents, Wanda and Cosmo.

Cosmo: She's the smart one!

Wanda: He's . . . well, he's cute, anyway.

Timmy: I'm going to give you the grand tour of my school... Dimmsdale Elementary. Do you go to school? If so, I'm sure you'll understand the kind of stuff I deal with. But having fairy godparents sure makes getting through the day a whole lot easier.

Timmy: Hmm. Before I take anyone on a tour of the entire school, I need to be able to go places without being seen.

Cosmo: Why don't you wish you were a little tiny bug?

Wanda: Oh dear, no. He could get smooshed!

Timmy: Good point. Hey! What if I wished I was invisible?

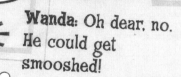

Wanda: That's a great idea, Sweetie!

Timmy: All right, then! I wish I were invisible!

VANISH!

—"Cool!"

Cosmo: AAAH! Where's that voice coming from? Timmy's bedroom is haunted!

Wanda: It's Timmy, Cosmo. He's invisible.

Timmy: Wait! If I don't show up for class, it'll look suspicious. I need a fake Timmy to stand in for me.

ZAP!

Timmy: Aw, no one is going to believe that's really me, you guys. It looks totally fake!

FAKE TIMMY

Cosmo: Sure they will! It's two-dimensional! Just like you!

Wanda: Here's a remote. When you want the fake Timmy to say something, just press one of these buttons.

Sure! Okay! Whatever you say!

I'm not fake at all. I'm really Timmy.

Crash Nebula rocks, dude!

You look pretty in a dress!

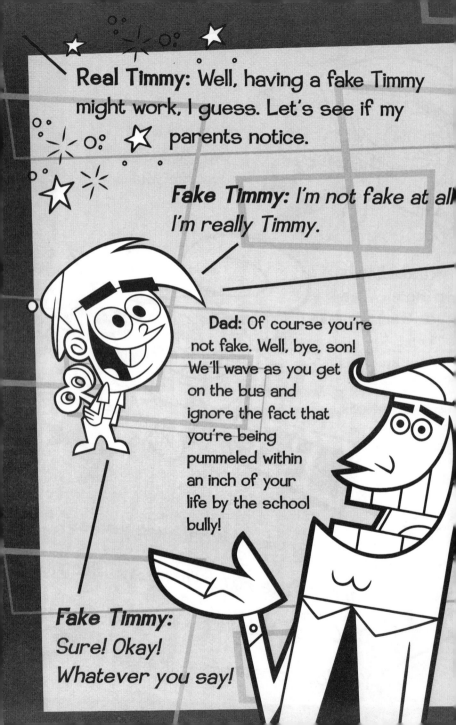

Wanda: Here comes the bus! We'll get the fake Timmy on board. You just make sure you get on the bus right behind him, Sweetie.

Cosmo: Hey! The fake Timmy keeps tripping. He's almost as clumsy as the real one!

Real Timmy: The popular kids sit in the back.

Bodyguard: This area is reserved.

Real Timmy: Here comes Trixie! Hey! Maybe I'll have the fake Timmy say something to her, since I never get up the nerve.

Trixie: Hello, unpopular kids! Hello, Veronica, my fellow popular friend who is, however, not as popular as me.

Fake Timmy: *You look pretty in a dress!*

Trixie: Did someone say something?

Veronica: I didn't hear anything.

Real Timmy: Check this out. Now we're in Mr. Crocker's class. Besides the fact that he doles out Fs right and left, he definitely suspects that I have fairy godparents.

Mr. Crocker: Timmy Turner! This biology paper you wrote is far too accomplished for you to have written it yourself. There is only one explanation: You had help from your fairy godparents! So I'm giving it an F- F for the fairies who helped you!

Fake Timmy: You look pretty in a dress!

Real Timmy: Wait! I didn't press any button!

Cosmo: Ooh. You're in big trouble now.

Wanda: Uh-oh. The clicker really is malfunctioning. Must be the batteries.

Mr. Crocker: The only way Turner could have seen me wearing that dress is with X-ray vision! That settles it! He *does* have fairy godparents! And I am going to find them with my secret heat-seeking fairy goggles!

Real Timmy: Oh, no. Mr. Crocker's going to detect my invisibility. I need a distraction! Quick! I wish there was a fire drill right now!

Real Timmy: That was close. Oh, great! Here comes Tootie! She's Vicky's little sister, and she's always trying to kiss me and stuff!

Cosmo: Eew! Girl cooties! Eeew!

Tootie: Hi, Timmy! Want to carry my books home from school for me today?

Fake Timmy: Sure! Okay! Whatever you say!

Real Timmy: Hey! This clicker thing is definitely not working!

Wanda: Hmm. Maybe there's a screw loose.

Cosmo: Are you talking about me?

Fake Timmy: Sure! Okay! Whatever you say!

A. J.: Timmy wants to take a quiz? It must be a sign of the apocalypse!

Mr. Crocker: The real Turner would never say that. There is only one explanation: This must be an imposter, and the real Turner must be invisible! I will expose him and his fairy godparents once and for all!

MWAH-HA-HA-HA-HA!

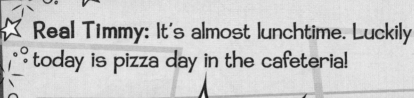

Real Timmy: It's almost lunchtime. Luckily today is pizza day in the cafeteria!

Attention students! As the latest budget was shot down once again by Dimmsdale's voters, pizza day has been cancelled. All we can afford to serve for lunch is . . . thin, watery gruel. Except the popular kids will get to choose their very own gourmet meal.

The Cafeteria

Real Timmy: This is the cafeteria. The popular kids sit over there.

Where the popular kids sit

Real Timmy: And everyone else sits over there.

Where everyone else sits

Trixie: Oh, there you are, Timmy Turner. I am doing a story about popularity for the school paper, and I need to interview a **total loser**. I may want to interview you later.

Real Timmy: Great. I get detention even when I'm not here.

Mr. Crocker: Once I get Turner into my detention class, I will expose his nefarious attempts to hide his fairy godparents from me!

Real Timmy: So now for the great unknown: the girls' bathroom! I can't believe I'm finally going to see what they do in there all the time!

Real Timmy: Welcome to gym class. This is usually not one of my favorite periods of the day . . .

Cosmo: Is that because you're really uncoordinated?

Real Timmy: Uh, a little more support here, please?

Wanda: Watch out for that ball, Sweetie.

Chester: Dude. Did you see that? The ball just changed direction in midair—almost like it bounced off something invisible.

Fake Timmy: *Crash Nebula rocks, dude!*

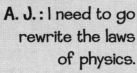**A. J. :** I need to go rewrite the laws of physics.

Real Timmy: Well, it's the official end of the school day. But not for me—I mean, the fake me. Mr. Crocker gave the fake me detention, remember? As you can see, the place gets pretty deserted around here after the final bell rings.

Real Timmy: Uh-oh. I just remembered Vicky is supposed to pick me up after school today. She's going to kill me if she has to wait for me to finish detention.

Real Timmy: Hey! I'll just send the fake Timmy home with *her*, and I'll go to detention! I wish I weren't invisible any more!

POOF!

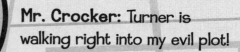

Mr. Crocker: Turner is walking right into my evil plot!

I know perfectly well that he is not the real Timmy Turner, but is a flimsily constructed duplicate fabricated by . . . his fairy godparents!

With this net I will capture the fake Turner and expose his ploy. Then I will finally be believed and will assume the reins of the New World Order!

MWAH-HA-HA-HA-HA-HA AAAAAA!!

Mr. Crocker:
I've got you now, Turner!

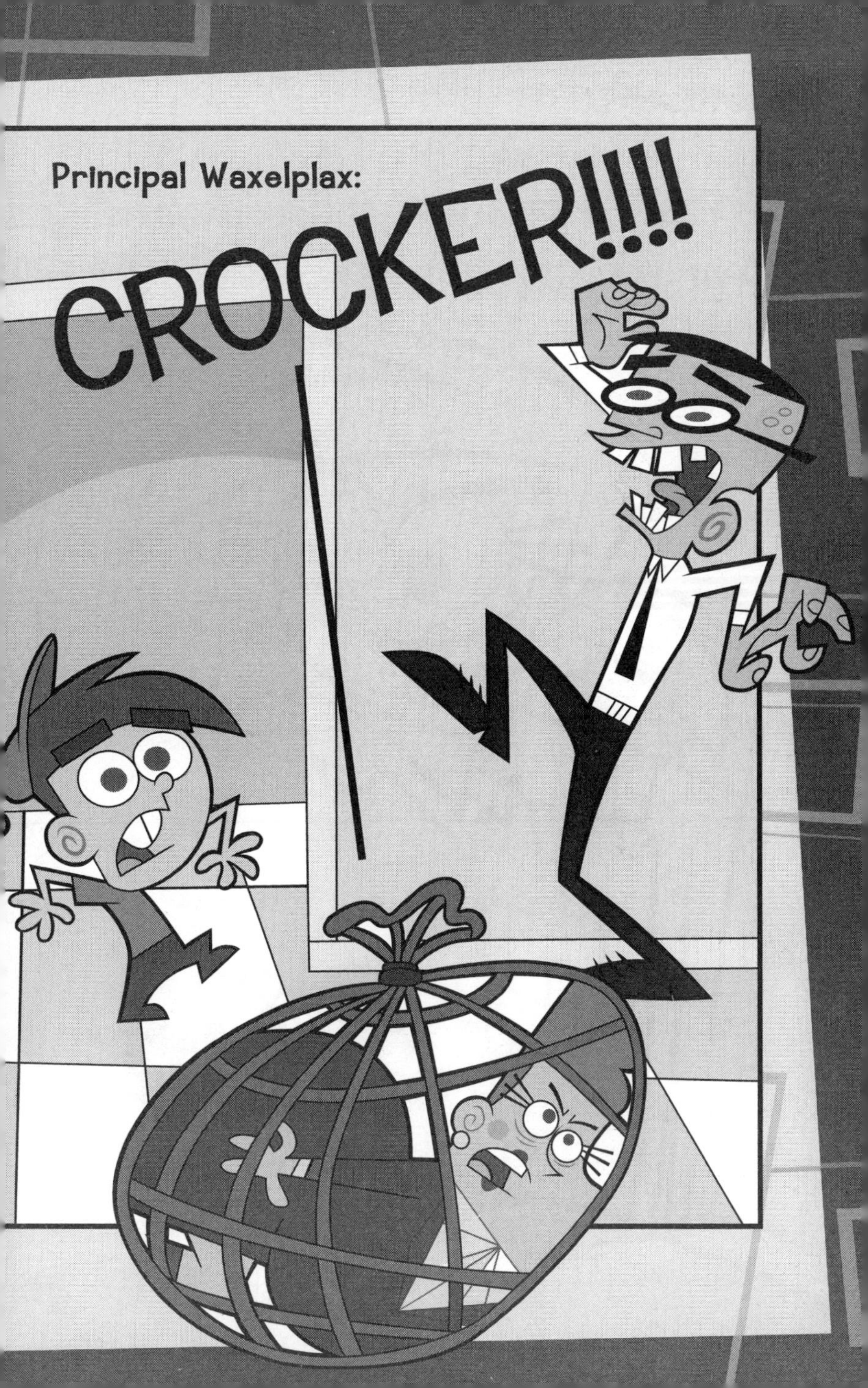
Principal Waxelplax:
CROCKER!!!!!

Real Timmy: Well, that concludes the tour of my school. Hey! I wonder what Vicky's doing with the fake Timmy right now.

Vicky: And after you walk Doidle, there's a pile of dirty laundry for you to do! Got that, Twerp?

Fake Timmy:

Sure! Okay! Whatever you say!
Sure! Okay! Whatever you say!
Sure! Okay! Whatever you say!
Sure! Okay! Whatever you say!
Sure! Okay! Whatever you say!
Sure! Okay! Whatever you say!
Sure! Okay! Whatever you say!
Sure! Okay! Whatever you say!
Sure! Okay! Whatever you say!
Sure! Okay! Whatever you say!
Sure! Okay! Whatever you say!

Real Timmy: I'm glad you came along with me today. As you can see, school isn't always the greatest place when you're me-but I'm not complaining.

Having fairy godparents certainly makes it more interesting.
Only eight more years to go!
Right, guys?